Let's Move O

The International Edition of Let's Make A Move!

By Beverly D. Roman

This book is dedicated to my children.

Dear Parents,

I have experienced moving overseas with children, and I understand how challenging international relocations are for families. I encourage you to work through this book's activities with your children to help them develop positive feelings about the move. By working closely with your children you will have a better understanding about how they are feeling and be able to help them adjust to a new home and community.

LET'S MOVE OVERSEAS was written to help children learn about their new country and deal with their feelings about moving. Safety tips, ways to maintain friendships and family traditions and Internet sites (page 9) are included. I hope that the messages and activities within these pages serve to help your children as you move overseas.

I wish you and your family all the best.

Sincerely,

Beverly D. Roman

Illustrated by Michael J. Cadieux

BR Anchor Publishing, Wilmington, North Carolina USA

My full name is: ______________________

I am ____ **years old.**

My father's name is: ______________________

My mother's name is: ______________________

Hi! I'm Thomas. My sister Isabella and I are moving. If you are moving too, this book will make it more fun.

List your friends' names and addresses here so you can write to them after you move.

____
name
____
E-mail
____
address
____

____
postal code, country

____
name
____
E-mail
____
address
____

____
postal code, country

____
name
____
E-mail
____
address
____

____
postal code, country

Printed in Canada

ISBN 1-888891-16-5
Edited by Dalene Bickel
Cover and illustrations by Michael J. Cadieux

PICTURE CODE

a e i o u

C_m_ _l_ng w_th _s_b_ll_

_nd Th_m_s f_r _ m_v_ng

_dv_nt_r_. Th_s _s y_ _r f_n

_ct_v_ty b_ _k. _v_ryth_ng

y_ _ n_ _d t_ m_v_ t_ _

n_w c_ _ntry _s _ns_d_

th_s b_ _k. H_v_ f_n!

SHARE YOUR FEELINGS

Lots of children are moving just like you. Ask your parents to tell you about the new country and be sure to share your feelings with them.

Fill in the name of your country every time you see • ______________________.

Dad: *"Thomas, Isabella, we want you to know that we are moving to a country called •* ______________________.

Thomas: *"I don't want to move."*

Isabella: *"I don't want to leave my friends."*

Dad: *"Mom and I know that you feel sad about leaving your friends, but we will help you to make new friends in •* ______________________ *."*

Mom: *"Dad and I are going to answer your questions and help you to learn about the country and the exciting places we will visit."*

Let's talk about your feelings.

I felt ______________________ when I learned I was moving.

We are moving because ______________________

I am most worried about ______________________

____

Things I will miss the most are ______________________

____

People I will miss the most include______________________

____

Ways I am going to help my family have a good move:

______________________ ______________________

______________________ ______________________

I would like to talk to my parents about:

____

____

____

______________________.

WORD SCRAMBLE

Dad and I think it is a good idea to write down your friends' addresses so you will be able to send them letters.
I will tell Jane and Sara about my new country.
I'll want my friends to send me E-mail.

Write your friends' addresses on page 2. Write your address on the cards on page 32 to give to your friends.

nstructions: Unscramble the words to find some of the things you might want your riends to do after you move. The answers are at the bottom of the page.

ritwe ot em ___ ___ ___ ___ ___ ___ ___ ___ ___

dens lmEia ___ ___ ___ ___ ___ ___ ___ ___ ___

dens curtpsei ___ ___ ___ ___

___ ___ ___ ___ ___ ___ ___ ___

eb ypahp ___ ___ ___ ___ ___ ___ ___

nktih fo em ___ ___ ___ ___ ___ ___ ___ ___ ___

write to me, send E-mail, send pictures, be happy, think of me

MY FRIENDS

Name
Name
Name
Let's make a scrapbook with pictures of our friends to take with us.
Let's give pictures of ourselves to our friends too.

What I like to do best with my friends.

____

____

____

MEMORIES

Here is a page to paste pictures and favorite objects from the school, city and home you are leaving. You can share these with your new friends after you move.

PLACES TO SEE

Thomas and Isabella, here are brochures with information about our new city and country. You can see the exciting places that we will visit.

Color code your family! When you travel wear the same color shirt, hat or something to distinguish yourselves. Always pick a place to meet your family in case you should become separated.

Instructions: Mark the places you might visit. In the blank space, write what you think you will see there.

_____ Museum ____

_____ Zoo ____

_____ Park ____

_____ Mountains ____

_____ Beach ____

_____ Historical Site ____

_____ Government Center ____

_____ Capital City ____

Other places to visit ____

____

____

LEARN ABOUT YOUR COUNTRY

Here are informative and fun Internet sites that Isabella and Thomas are going to search with their parents. Ask your parents to help you learn about such things as the geography, weather and language of your new country. Have fun!

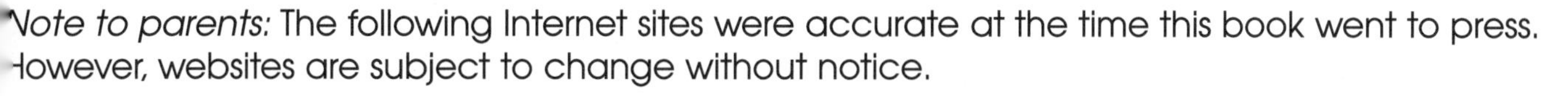

Note to parents: The following Internet sites were accurate at the time this book went to press. However, websites are subject to change without notice.

- **National Geographic** http://www.nationalgeographic.com
  Learn about the world, enjoy fun games, select a penpal and go on "Family Xpeditions."
- **The Weather Channel** http://www.weather.com
  Discover the weather conditions in your new city and around the world. Use this site to answer the questions on page 11.
- **Berlitz** http://www.berlitz.com/kidtalk/default.htm
  "Kid Talk" with games for kids and tips for parents. A place for the whole family to explore the exciting world of languages. Offers jokes, games, a coloring activity and language books and tapes for children.
- **Internet Public Library, Youth Division** http://www.ipl.org/youth
  Click on "Our World" to learn about religions, languages, geography and world culture.
- **Searchopolis** http://searchopolis.com
  Searchopolis is a filtered search engine for children and teenagers. Fast Find categories are especially helpful.
- **Kids' Space** http://www.kids-space.org
  Perform a country search and visit KS Connection to make friends all over the world.
- **Virtual Tourist** http://www.vtourist.com/vt
  Explore the world and the people living there. Also learn about currencies, time zones, calendars, directions and more.

OTHER RESOURCES: BOOKS BY BR ANCHOR PUBLISHING

Let's Make A Move! (young children)
Footsteps Around the World (teens)
Relocation 101 (domestic)
Home Away From Home (international)

See our books on the web at: **http://www.branchor.com**

YOUR PLACE IN THE WORLD

Instructions: Ask your parents to help you find your new country on this map and mark it. There are questions in this book to help you to learn about • ________________ and what it is like to live there. You can also find country information using the Internet sites on page 9.

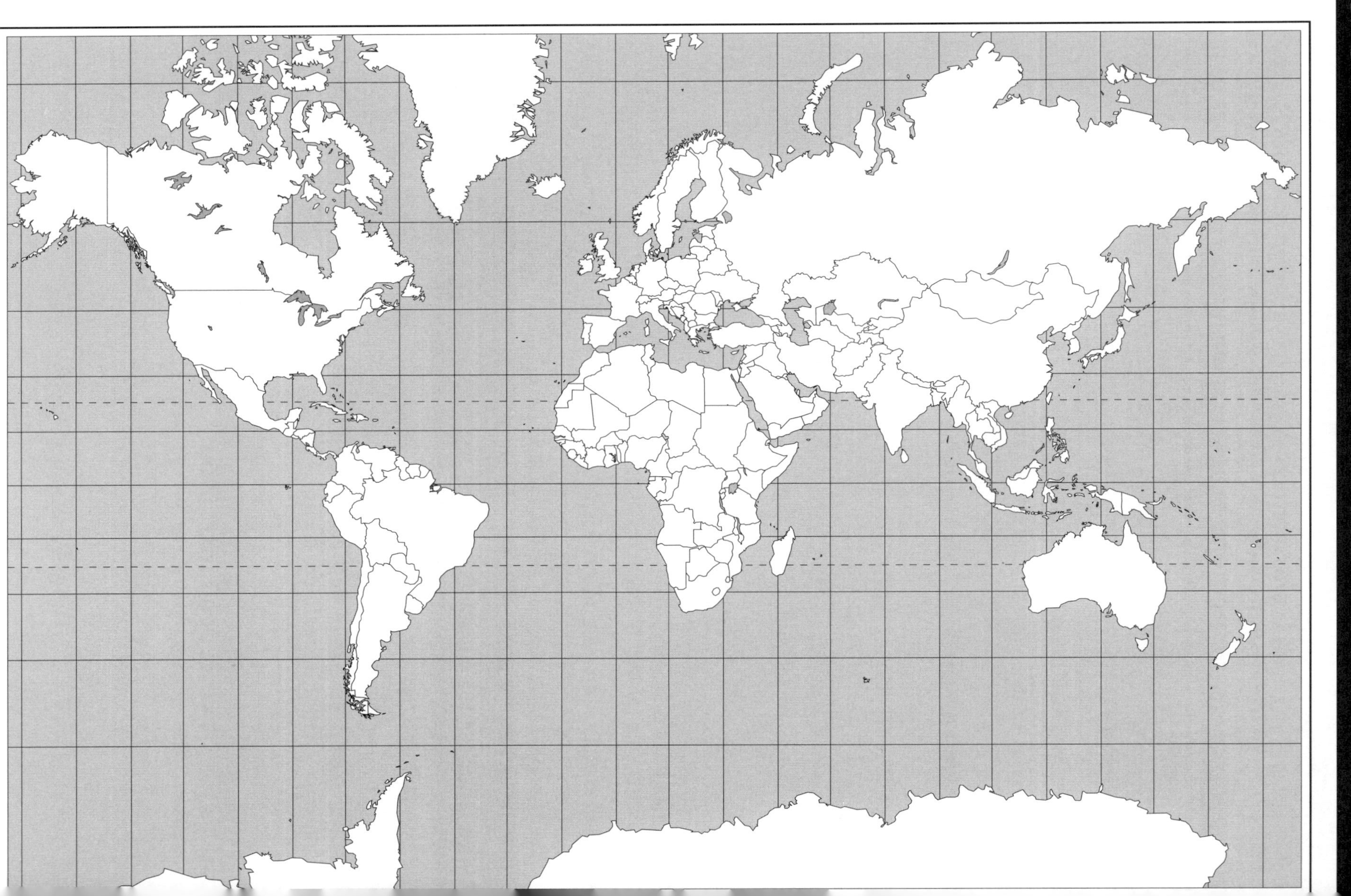

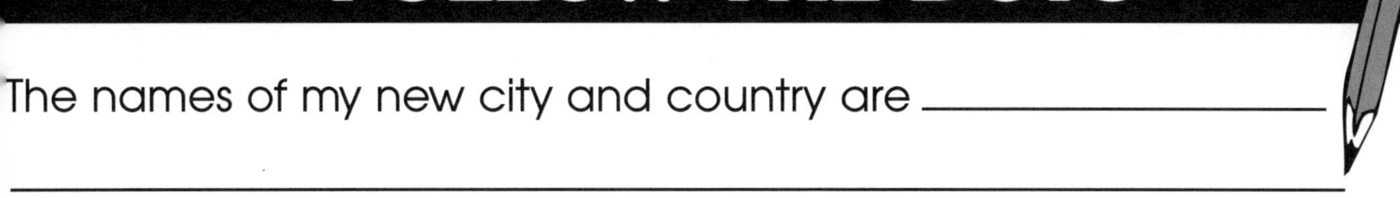

FOLLOW-THE-DOTS

The names of my new city and country are ____________________

____

The weather will be like this: ______________________________.

(Examples: hot, humid, rainy and dry)

It will take ______ hours to travel to • ______________________.

In • ______________________ I will use ______________ for money.

I will have to dial ______________ on the telephone for emergencies.

The temperature can be as high as ________ and as low as ________.

Follow the dots to see how people often travel to other countries.

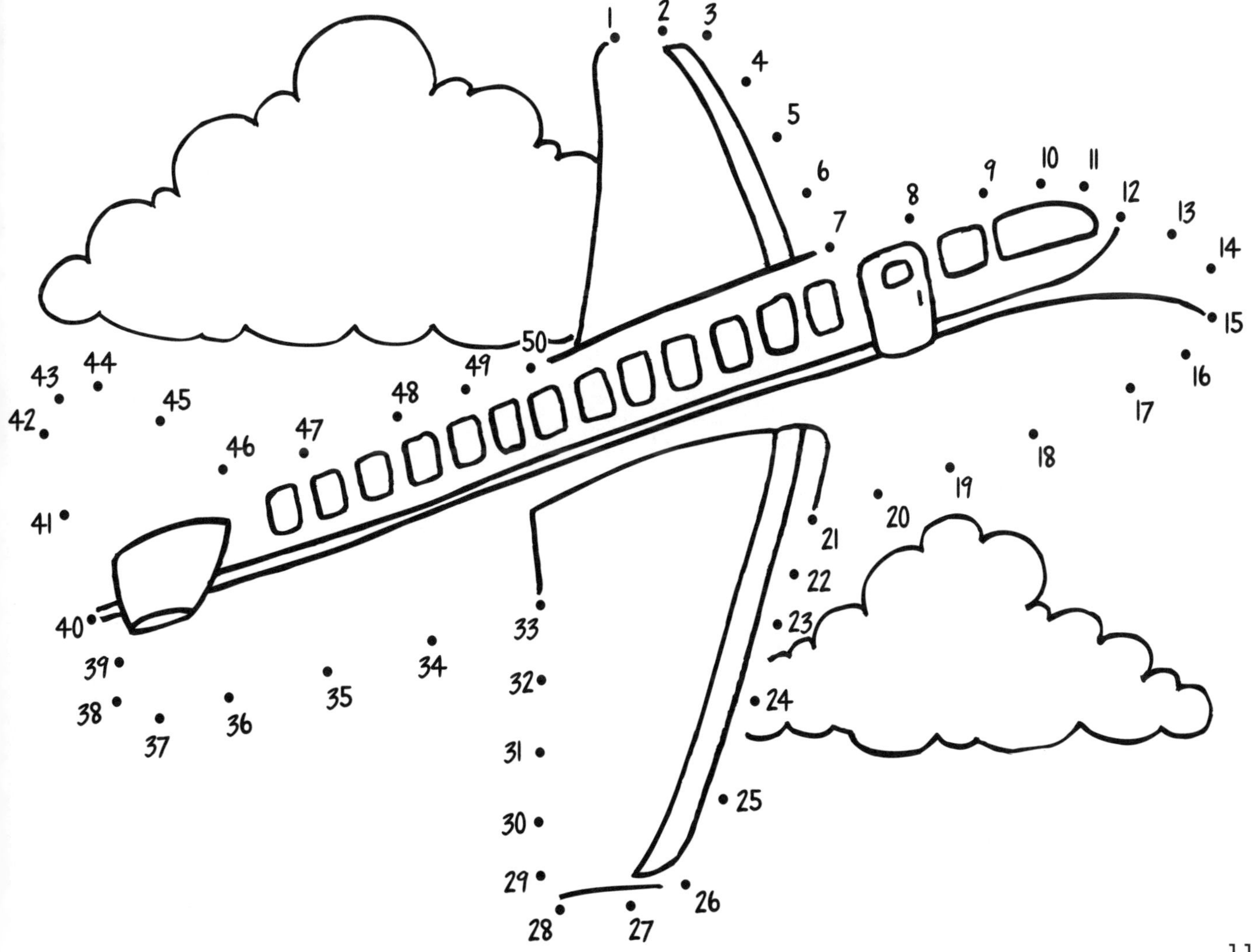

FILL-IN-THE-BLANKS

Fill in the empty blanks below, then color the picture of Thomas and Isabella with their friends.

The largest city in my country is ______________________________

The countries that border my new country are ______________________________

____

____

My country is famous for ______________________________

The sports that are played in my city are called:

Soccer______________________ Golf______________________

Tennis ______________________ Track ______________________

Gymnastics______________________ Other______________________

Here are some of the places we will see in

. ______________________ .

LEARNING THE CULTURE

In your new country you will meet people who may talk or act differently than you. Let's write down what some of those things might be.

This is the way people greet each other: ______________________________

____

____.

It is nice to say____.

It is not nice to say____.

People speak this language______________________________________.

The type of clothing that is worn includes ___________________________

____.

The music we will hear is _______________________________________.

Typical foods are____

____.

Special holidays or festivals are __________________________________

____

____.

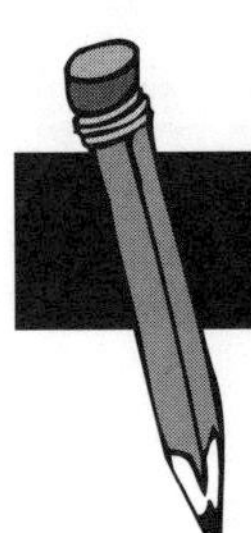

LEARNING THE LANGUAGE

Instructions: Draw your new country in this space.

It is important to learn how to speak the language of your new country in case you need help or directions. Ask your parents to help you write and learn to say these important words.

Hello ______________________________

Goodbye ______________________________

Please ______________________________

Thank you ______________________________

My name is ______________________________

Excuse me. ______________________________

Help! ______________________________

My telephone number is ______________________________

My address is ______________________________

Where is the bathroom? ______________________________

I am hungry. ______________________________

I am thirsty. ______________________________

I am lost. ______________________________

I am sick. ______________________________

Do you speak English? ______________________________

I do not understand. ______________________________

Other words: ______________________________

DRAW YOUR NEW HOUSE

Instructions: Here is a picture of Thomas and Isabella's new house. Ask your parents for a picture or a description of your new house and draw it in the space below.

What do you think you will like best about your new home?

____

____

____

ANIMAL PICTURE CODE

Would you like to see pictures of our new house?

Instructions: Fill in the blanks using the animal code.

a e i o u

Th__m__s __nd __s__b__ll__ __r__ sh__w__ng

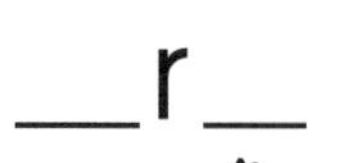

th__ __r fr__ __nds p__ct__r__s __f th__ __r

n__w h__ __s__. D__ y__ __ h__v__

p__ct__r__s __f y__ __r n__w h__m__?

CROSSWORD PUZZLE

There are people coming to see our house. If they like it, they will buy it for their family. Please help Dad and me by putting your toys and clothes away.

Instructions: Fill in the spaces with the things that Thomas and Isabella are putting away or doing to make their rooms tidy.

2 DOWN

3 DOWN

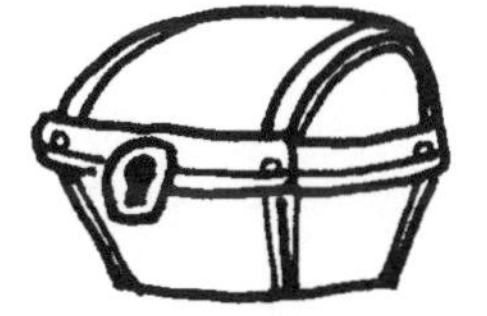

4 DOWN

1 ACROSS

5 DOWN

3 ACROSS

6 DOWN

5 ACROSS

9 DOWN

7 ACROSS

8 ACROSS

10 DOWN

PLAN A TRIP TO THE PARK

While a new family looks at their house, Isabella and Thomas are planning a trip to the park with their parents. They are going to meet some of their friends there too.

Instructions: Write down what you would like to do in the park.

____

____

____

____

____

Isabella and Thomas are packing a picnic lunch to take to the park. You might like to plan a picnic too. On the next page there are suggestions for lunch.

PACK A PICNIC LUNCH

Instructions: Write down the things you want to pack in your lunch.

I am going to make a sandwich to put in my lunch. What are you going to pack?

I am going to make the Trail Mix because it is my favorite snack.

______________________ ______________________

______________________ ______________________

______________________ ______________________

Try this fun snack idea.

Trail Mix

4 cups dry granola cereal

$^1/_3$ cup nuts

$^1/_2$ cup sunflower seeds

$^1/_4$ cup raisins

$^2/_3$ cup dried fruit

Put the mix in plastic bags for your trip!

Other lunch suggestions:

- ☐ pudding
- ☐ fresh fruit
- ☐ fruit or health bars
- ☐ jello

What is your favorite lunch?

____

____

____

SEEK AND FIND

Instructions: Look carefully to find the "hidden" objects in the picture. Some items are food you would take on a picnic, and some are animals or objects that are in the park.

- Apple
- Star
- Sandwich
- Squirrel
- Key
- Book
- Baseball Mitt
- Frog
- 6 Crayons
- Banana
- Pencil
- Lunch bag
- 3 Birds
- Tree
- Duck
- Seesaw
- Fork
- Horseshoe
- Swing
- Whistle
- Butterfly
- Baseball
- Sliding Board
- Acorn

LIST YOUR CHORES

Instructions: Here is a list of a few chores to do before moving. Put a mark by each chore when you finish it and add whatever else you need to do. Color the picture of Thomas and Isabella packing.

Return library books __________ Clean out my school locker ________

Return toys I borrowed ________ Pack a matching shirt for trips ______

Other ____

____

SEEK-A-WORD

Instructions: Search the puzzle for the items that you may want to put in your backpack. Look across, down, backward and diagonally.

Mom said we should put some of our special things in our backpacks. Let's plan what we will take along on our trip.

BOOKS
GAMES
TABLET
PHOTOS
PENCIL
CARDS
MUSIC
HEADSET
CAMERA
ADDRESSES
CRAYONS

C	M	C	B	O	O	K	S	H	T
A	T	E	L	B	A	T	H	P	S
M	A	C	K	G	A	M	E	S	E
E	V	I	T	I	L	N	A	C	S
R	Y	S	L	E	C	O	D	R	S
A	O	U	E	I	K	X	S	A	E
C	H	M	L	I	D	N	E	Y	R
W	S	O	T	O	H	P	T	O	D
K	U	D	H	P	E	N	A	N	D
C	A	R	D	S	N	S	O	S	A

COLOR AND PACK

Instructions: Color the picture any way you wish.
Add a toy that you want to pack.

AN ADVENTURE MAZE

Instructions: Here are some of the sites you will see in other countries. See if you can find your way from the airport to your new home.

SEEK-A-WORD

Instructions: Search the puzzle for the words of things to do in your new city. Look across, down, backward and diagonally.

SWIM
LEARN
CLIMB
PLAY
HIKE
ADVENTURE
SCHOOL
BIKE
RUN
DISCOVER
TRAVEL
SWING

WRITE ABOUT YOUR SCHOOL

Instructions: Fill in the lines on the backpack with things you will need on your first day of school.

My new school is called

____.

My room number is ________________.

My teacher's name is

____.

My school colors are

____

____.

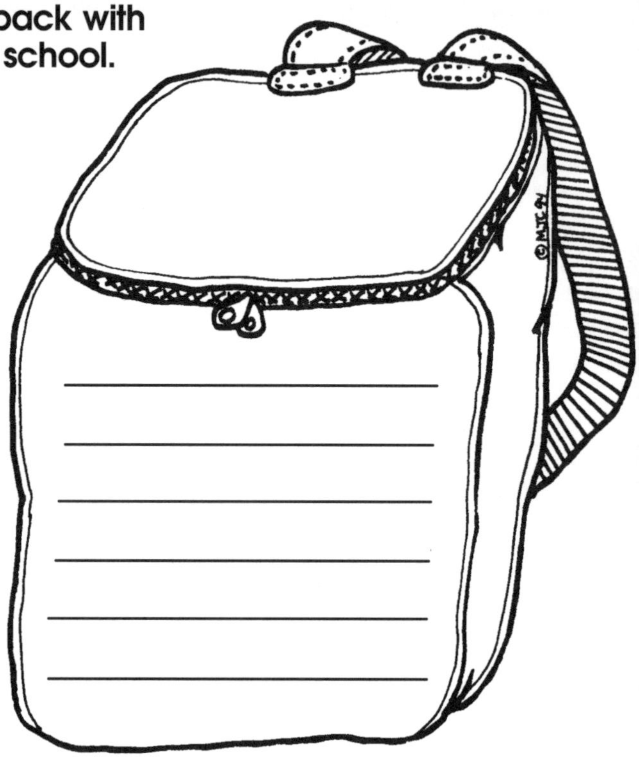

____

____

____

____

____

____

Many schools have the following features. Which ones will you find at your school?

- ☐ cafeteria
- ☐ flag pole
- ☐ baseball diamond
- ☐ soccer field
- ☐ library
- ☐ swings

Write down what else will be at your school.

____

____

____

____

____

LEARN YOUR WAY TO SCHOOL

Thomas and Isabella, Mom and I do not want you to get lost. It is very important that you always go to the bus stop and come home using the streets that we practiced.

BUS STOP

BUS

Instructions: Write down all the important things you need to know in the blank spaces.

My new bus / train number is: ____________________ .

My bus / train stop is on this street: ____________________ .

I leave for my stop at this time: ____________________ .

I come home from my stop at this time: ____________________ .

I take these streets on the way to and from my bus / train stop:

____

____

____ .

These are the only people I may ride to school and home with:

____

____ .

Contact telephone numbers. Carry these with you until you remember them.

My home ____________________

My mother's work ____________________

My father's work ____________________

A neighbor or friend ____________________

COLOR BY NUMBER

Instructions: Use the number code at the bottom of the page. Color Thomas' and Isabella's clothes the colors you like.

1 – LIGHT BLUE	3 – YELLOW	5 – ORANGE	7 – GRAY	9 – DARK BLUE
2 – RED	4 – BLACK	6 – GREEN	8 – BROWN	10 – PURPLE

FILL-IN-THE-BLANKS FOR SAFETY

Instructions: Here are safety tips for your new home.
If you need help to fill in the spaces, ask someone in your family.

Where are these items located?

Fire Extinguisher ______________________

First Aid Kit

____

Flashlight / Torch

____

Emergency Exits

____

____

____

Smoke Detectors

______________________ ______________________

______________________ ______________________

If I need help, my parents say I can ask these people:

______________________ ______________________

______________________ ______________________

My new home address is: ______________________

______________________.

Rules to follow ...

Look both ways before crossing a street.

Always cross streets at the crosswalks.

Obey traffic lights and signs.

Know the streets that are safe to travel.

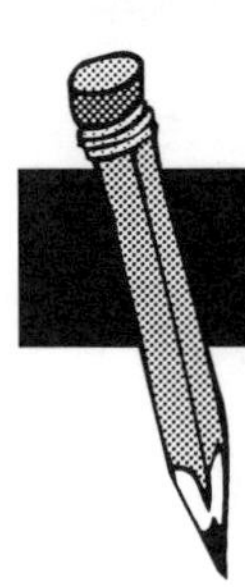

THINK HAPPY THOUGHTS

Here are suggestions to help you enjoy your new country. Good luck and be happy.

Special family traditions or holidays that we will celebrate in our new home:

____

____

______________________________.

I am excited about doing ______________________________

______________________________ in my new city.

When I am excited or unhappy about something, I know I can share my feelings with: ______________________________

____

______________________________.

The best part about my new school is: ______________________________

______________________________.

I am going to write to these people and tell them about my new home:

______________ ______________

______________ ______________

______________ ______________

My parents say that I am special because:

____

____

____

____

______________________________.

CLAP! CLAP! CLAP! CLAP!

Congratulations! You did a great job!

PICTURE/WORD MATCH

Instructions: Draw a line from each word to the correct picture.

TRUCK

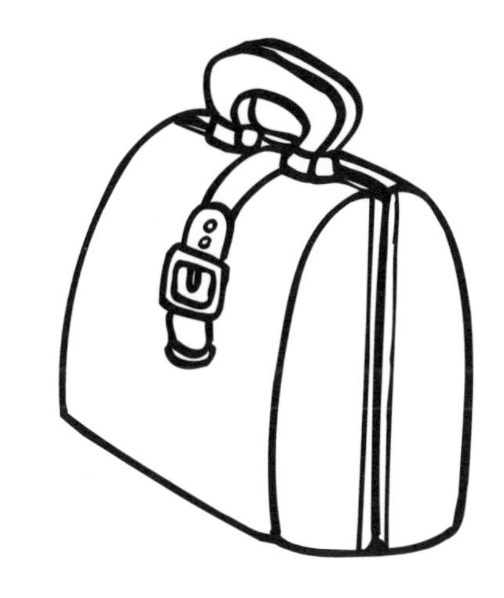

CAT

BASEBALL
BAT/GLOVE

FISH

SUITCASE

BEAR

DOG

YOUR NEW ADDRESS

Instructions: Write down your new address and then cut the cards out for your friends.

name

E-mail

address

postal code, country

name

E-mail

address

postal code, country

name

E-mail

address

postal code, country

name

E-mail

address

postal code, country